LORENZO

By

Luis M. A. Fernandes

I would like to dedicate this book to my wife Fatima and my daughter Melissa, who encouraged me to write this book.

CONTENTS

ACKNOWLEDGMENTS

Writing is my passion so I am happy to have written this book. I would like to thank my daughter for helping me research about the island of Madeira. I would also like to extend my heartfelt thanks to Kindle publications for publishing my book *Lorenzo*.

CHAPTER 1

Nourished by our creator
We blossom into his likeness and image
Like fruit ripened that falls to the ground
Life's journey comes to a sudden end
Dust were we
Dust we return to
Dust unto dust we turn into.

Sitting on the Camara de Lobos beach, a little fishing village in Western Madeira in Portugal, facing the vast imposing sea, Lorenzo wondered what the future was going to be like for him and the rest of the family. He spent the better part of his life since his childhood near the seafront with his father, besides attending school and later training himself under his father's supervision in boat building. Over the years Lorenzo established a very special bond with the sea. The sea was, and still is, a second home for him. The sea and everything associated with the sea is a passion beyond compare. He would spend his free time just sitting on the beach and staring at the sea. He was totally fascinated with it, totally in love with it like a lover would be.

But today Lorenzo is in a confused state of mind, not knowing what to think or make of it. He is terribly upset but not angry, confused but not discouraged, shaken but not weakened. He keeps telling himself that he has to be strong and continue to have a strong faith with his lover, the sea. He cannot give up now. He has come a long way. Now there is no turning back. Something within his conscience speaks with him to continue loving the sea and it will reward him beyond his imagination. He decides then and there to listen to the voice speaking to his conscience.

Back home there was commotion as the time for the funeral was closing in and no one seemed to know where to find Lorenzo. People who gathered at his residence for the funeral volunteered to search for him. Catherine Pelagio is the sister of Lorenzo's best friend Francisco, and knew best where to find him. She ran straight to the beach, followed by Francisco, and found him just staring at the sea. Catherine Pelagio, who reached Lorenzo first, dropped herself on the sandy beach on her knees, gasping for breath, followed by Francisco, who reminded him of the funeral. That's when Lorenzo came to his senses and the three of them raced home. From a distance he saw a crowd of people gathered around his house offering condolences and sympathies to the family members. Lorenzo entered the house and stood in silence, still trying to come to terms with his father's death. He tried to hold back his emotions and tears but could not do so for long and wept bitterly, for he loved his father very dearly, as he did the rest of the family members. In fact Lorenzo by nature is a very compassionate and caring person, always willing to help and be of service to others.

Staring at his father's coffin, Lorenzo started recollecting past memories, how he, as a child, accompanied his father to attend the church service every Sunday; he taught him catechism to prepare him for the first holy communion and later on for confirmation, enrolled him at school and guided him throughout his life to gain the much-needed experience to face life with confidence backed by wisdom, knowledge, and insight. After school Lorenzo would join his father even as a child and observe him at work at the boat building yard, observing and learning all the time. He developed a passion for boat building at a very young age and wanted to be a fine craftsman like his father. Antonio Joao Ribeiro observed his son carefully and realised that his son, too, wanted to follow in his footsteps.

But Alberto Joao Ribeiro wanted his son to study well at school and at university like most parents do, acquire a good qualification to secure his future instead of following in the footsteps of his father. Within himself Lorenzo was in turmoil to make up his mind, whether to make known his desire of boat building to his father. Lorenzo continued to accompany his father to the yard. One day Lorenzo picked up enough courage and made known his desire of boat building to his father. Alberto Joao Ribeiro looked at his son with compassion and nodded his head in approval. Lorenzo rushed into the comforting arms of his father as tears of joy rolled down his cheeks.

Alberto Joao Ribeiro continued, saying, "My son, I have granted you your wish, would you grant me mine?"

"Of course I will," replied Lorenzo obediently.

"I will turn you into a great craftsman in boat building by transferring all my skills to you without holding back anything, provided you promise me to fulfil my dream of you acquiring a university degree in any discipline of your choice. I will leave no stone unturned to finance your education. All you have to do is to study. I have a very sentimental attachment to this trade since our ancestors for the last five generations have earned their living by following the twin profession of fishing and boat building. They all prospered, and so did we by following these professions."

Lorenzo hugged his father, and being an obedient son, agreed to his father's request.

And here is Lorenzo, staring at his dead father lying in a coffin; he died at sea, in a ferocious storm, the sea he trusted all his life which nurtured him, helped him and his family to prosper. It was time for the funeral. The entire Camara de Lobos village turned out for the funeral in a silent procession proceeding to the church of **Sao Sebastiao**, Camara de Lobos, showing solidarity with the bereaved family. Behind the scenes Catherine volunteered wholeheartedly to extend help and support to the bereaved family by taking care of all the arrangements. The whole village was full of praise and admiration for Catherine, especially Lorenzo's family, who watched and admired her skills and ability to manage everything with grace, displaying great inner strength and courage.

*

Alberto Joao Ribeiro, survived by his wife Isabela, sons Lorenzo Joao Ribeiro and Antonio Joao Ribeiro, and daughter Belinda, was the fifth generation seafarer using the Caravel that could sail against the wind which Dom Henrique (Prince Henry the Navigator, youngest son of Dom Joao I, King John I of Portugal and Philippa of Lancaster) designed and commissioned seafarers to discover new routes to India and China. Henry the Navigator was a driving force in the discovery of the world beyond the established trade routes. Alberto Joao Ribeiro's ancestors began their seafarer's journey nearing the end of the fourteenth century.

Lorenzo's ancestors were adventurous and courageous. They all loved the sea that gave them the much-needed confidence to venture into it and learn more about it. With the passage of time, it became their second home as they had to spend better part of their life at sea. They invested in their sons all the knowledge and experience they had acquired over the years so that they may follow in their footsteps later to earn a livelihood, since that was the most sought-after profession that was available in that era, which paid well, but the risk involved was much greater.

Lorenzo's ancestors progressed well in their profession. Since they were fishermen by profession, this gave them the added advantage of working at sea. The more time they spent at sea, the more they learnt about the mechanisms of the ship and the behavioural pattern of the sea. They were sought after for their expertise, experience, and vast knowledge of the sea and of course, honesty. This placed them in a very favourable position to remain employed till a ripe age.

They climbed the success ladder from humble beginnings as crew members. They had the privilege to participate in the various stages of exploration at sea. Alberto Joao Ribeiro Senior succeeded in realising his childhood dream of becoming the Ship Captain. One year later he died at sea in a ferocious storm. He was buried at the local church in his village.

CHAPTER 2

Realities of life presses hard to move on,
Day or night sunset or early morn,
Run the rat race called survival of the fittest,
Playing your cards right will make you the mightiest.

Lorenzo has now to fill the void left by his father's death and move forward, focusing his full attention on the many responsibilities that he has to shoulder as the elder son. He has to fulfil the promise he made to his father besides taking care of the family, his mother, brother, and sister. Overcoming the grief of his father's tragic death at sea was not easy for the family, especially for Lorenzo. Lorenzo thought over his life ahead and decided that the best way to honour his father was not to grieve for him, but to fulfil his father's wish, and the promise he made to his father before his death. He decided to pursue his twin professions by acquiring a marine engineering degree and continuing with the traditional boat building business activity to fulfil his father's wishes while his father was alive, to preserve the centuries-old craftsmanship which would secure the traditional fishermen's future and livelihood in a competitive commercial fishing industry. His brother Antonio decided to be a Business Administrator and sister Belinda decided to follow the medical profession in Gynaecology. Lorenzo renamed the Boat Building Yard to 'A.J. Rebeiro Boat Building Yard'.

*

Catherine Pelagio is the only daughter of a rich merchant named Stefano Pelagio. Grapes (for wine), grain, and sugarcane were grown on Madeira Island from the very beginning. The local landowners flourished in their trade by exporting the local (produce) commodities, especially white gold and wine, which was in great demand, and later on importing commodities like gold, ivory, and pepper from the West African coast. Various other contingents of settlers arrived. They invested in sugarcane and irrigation projects, and later performed the role of landowner, merchant and financier.

Catherine Pelagio and Lorenzo's family had maintained a very cordial relationship for generations together.

Stefano Pelagio has continued with the age-old tradition of his ancestors. When Stefano Pelagio's ancestors first came to Madeira from Italy, they brought with them their business acumen, farming know-how, implements, and wealth, besides experience and expertise to start a new beginning. They surveyed the island by their vessel in search of a safe place to land and saw smoke above the island, and knew at once that the island may be inhabited by people. They anchored the vessel and rowed by boat in the direction of the smoke to explore the island, not knowing what they would encounter.

They took with them two of their ship crewmen who had visited the island several times in the past when they anchored their ship for rest and repair, and left the other crew on the vessel to wait for their return. Stefano Pelagio's ancestors travelled on foot with their crewmen in the dense wooded island, camping and resting. After a few days of travel they climbed what looked like a mountain (the modern day Camara de Lobos), but they were disappointed to see no human habitation anywhere around, which they hoped for. After exploring the mountain they decided to settle there for the time being, worn out and totally exhausted from their journey.

As they began climbing down the mountain to return to their vessel they noticed, once again, smoke coming out of the valley below. They had passed sleepless nights while exploring the island, taking turns to keep watch during the night while sleeping and resting. What they needed most was a bath, food, and a good night's sleep. Excitedly, they hurried down the mountain, hoping against hope to find their destination before the sunset. As they climbed down the mountain they lost sight of the smoke; one of the crewmen came to their rescue saying not to worry but to follow him, and he led them right near to the source of the smoke in the valley.

They hid themselves behind trees to scan the surroundings. They saw four traditional thatched cottages built around a wide open space by clearing the forest. For an hour there was no activity. Stefano Pelagio and the crew were not so sure anymore whether they did the right thing by coming down the mountain. They had to act swiftly before the sunset or else had to spend another night in the wilderness. On a densely wooded island like Madeira, it gets pitch dark before sunset. Just then, they could hear human voices but could not understand what was being said.

Stefano Pelagio took the bold step by marching towards the traditional thatched cottages to the great surprise of his crew. He stopped a few metres before the entrance of the cottage, not knowing what to do next. He could hear the murmuring of voices from inside the cottage. He realised that maybe the inhabitants of the cottage were equally confused and afraid to find strangers at their doorstep. He decided to make his move. Not knowing what language to speak, he said hello in Italian. "Is anybody home?" Nothing happened or moved. Again he said the same thing in Portuguese. "Is anybody at home?" Surprised, the cottage residents started talking among themselves in Portuguese and all the four cottage residents came out of their residences to welcome the strangers in their humble dwellings.

It was Lorenzo's ancestors who gave shelter to Stefano Pelagio's ancestors when they first arrived at Madeira, since they had nowhere to live. Lorenzo's ancestors were so kind and generous that they let them have one fully furnished cottage exclusively for them. Stefano Pelagio's ancestors stayed with Lorenzo's ancestors for one year since they had to start from scratch with a new life, a new beginning in a new country and environment. With full backing and moral support from Lorenzo's ancestors they fully integrated into Madeira's culture, customs, business, religion, food habits, etc., and reaped a good fortune by their sheer hard work, dedication, and honesty. Both the families developed a strong bonding over the years and stood beside each other on all occasions. This mutual bond of friendship has been passed on to generation after generation, and it continues to grow.

*

Lorenzo decided to qualify as a marine engineer to fulfil his father's dream and start his own venture in shipbuilding. His brother Antonio decided to qualify for a degree in Business Administration, and sister Belinda set her hopes high to specialise in Gynaecology. Now he has to shoulder multiple roles as a student and caretaker of the family in the absence of his father, manage the traditional boat building and repair yard, finance his and his younger sister and brother's education, besides managing all other family obligations. He sat and thought deeply of how to manage and meet all the challenges that lay ahead of him, which seemed impossible to achieve.

He decided to plan out the tasks he would have to do on a daily basis by allocating time to each of his activities, so that all activities would get proper attention and progress together. He enlisted the help and co-operation of his younger brother and sister, who were only too happy to oblige wholeheartedly. Lorenzo organised the daily work schedule between the three of them, allocating enough time to devote to their studies. Their mother Isabela shouldered the entire domestic household responsibilities, leaving the children free to carry on with their studies and daily tasks. All the local community were full of admiration and praise to see how Lorenzo's family managed to build their lives after the loss of their loving father without indulging in self-pity and discouragement.

Lorenzo's family set about rebuilding their shattered lives with determination and courage. Their adventurous nature helped them to bounce back from obscurity to great heights of success. That's the stuff they are made of. The academic year began and Lorenzo, together with his brother Antonio and Belinda, began in earnest their mission to accomplish their personal dream. Each one of them has a dream to fulfil. They know that they have to remain focused on their dream to achieve it, work hard for it, make sacrifices, be ready to face setbacks and disappointments, and continue to march towards their goal with renewed zeal till the dream is realised. Lorenzo's brother Antonio and Belinda had been brought up with a good moral education by their parents in a very closely knit family, as is the case for the majority of the families on Madeira.

Family plays a very vital role on Madeira. Strong family affiliation helps them to have a very affectionate relationship with all family members, including the extended family, which in turn provides continued social security. Aged members of the family are loved and cared for and in return they offer their services caring for the younger generations, teaching and inculcating good values in them that have been passed on for generations together.

Unemployed family members' needs are taken care of by those who are employed by pulling all their resources together to ensure that no family member feels neglected or uncared for. The scenario on Madeira is slowly but steadily changing for the better as schools, colleges, universities and institutes in different disciplines are opened throughout Madeira, catering to the needs of the ever-conscious present younger generation who want to take advantage of the facilities offered to better their prospects for a bright future ahead.

*

Today is the first day they begin a new chapter in their life, marching forward with confidence to acquire qualification, skills, and expertise in their respective discipline to carve out a better future for themselves, backed by all the family members' encouragement and support. As they were walking towards the bus stand, Lorenzo noticed from a distance a somewhat familiar face walking towards them from the opposite direction.

It was only when Lorenzo's sister waved to her and called her by name that Lorenzo realised who she was. Lorenzo stood stunned and speechless, staring at Catherine. She looked like an angel, the prettiest Catherine he had ever seen before. As he continued to stand speechless and motionless, Belinda measured up the prevailing situation and pinched her brother Lorenzo to bring him to his senses without drawing the attention of the others.

Once awakened he felt shy and embarrassed, and greeted Catherine with a beautiful smile, and she in turn greeted him with a handshake, wishing him success in his endeavour. She is the same Catherine who knew where to find Lorenzo on the day of his father's funeral when everybody from their village was looking for him. Catherine raced straight to the Camara de Lobos beach and found Lorenzo sitting and staring at the sea, completely lost in his thoughts, awakened by Catherine when she dropped herself on the beach next to Lorenzo, followed by Catherine's brother Francisco.

Belinda and her brother Antonia did most of the talking for the remaining part of their journey towards the university, while Catherine and Lorenzo sat behind Belinda and Antonio, lost in their own thoughts. This pin-drop silence was something they had never experienced before. For the first time since their childhood they felt uncomfortable and restless while they were together. By nature they are jolly, fun-loving, extrovert personalities.

They grew up together through their childhood, all four of them: Lorenzo, Catherine, Belinda, and Antonio. They were nicknamed the **Jolly Foursome** and were very popular. Occasionally Lorenzo and Catherine stole a glance from the corner of their eyes. What thoughts must be occupying their minds while they remain silent, waiting to see who will make the first move and break the silence between them?

As they were lost in their own thoughts in a different world, suddenly the bus came to a screeching halt and all passengers were thrown forward to avoid a direct collision with a bus at the crossroads. Lorenzo's timely reaction to the situation saved Catherine from being hurt badly. He saw the bus entering the crossroads without stopping and held Catherine back with his arm when the situation went out of control. Belinda and Antonio sustained minor injuries, though some passengers sustained serious injuries and had to be rushed to the hospital. The Jolly Foursome continued their journey and reached their destination.

Catherine was still shaken up. Lorenzo spoke for the first time and comforted her. She was fighting back her tears but could not hold them back. She burst out crying, not knowing why. Lorenzo wiped her tears and tried to calm her down. Catherine rolled both her hands on Lorenzo's cheek and with tears still in her eyes, thanked him for saving her from getting hurt with his presence of mind. She apologised for not speaking with him on the bus. She told Lorenzo for the first time in her life she felt too shy to speak with him. Every time she tried to speak with him while on the bus her lips would tremble. She could not understand what was happening to her. Lorenzo too was confused with her behaviour and could not understand what to make of it. The famous Jolly Foursome no longer seemed jolly.

CHAPTER 3

Privacy and your companionship I long for
To express my innermost feelings.
My soul delights with thoughts & past memories of you
Sleep evades me, restless I lie to see thee,
Make haste oh sweet morn with your radiant light
Usher in a new day, delight my soul, in my love, I pray.

At break time the Jolly Foursome sat together on the lush green lawns of the campus. Catherine now looked well poised and relaxed, though neither she nor Lorenzo made any move to talk. Sister Belinda and Antonio decided to leave Lorenzo and Catherine alone by excusing themselves to visit the university library. Lorenzo took courage and asked Catherine politely whether she was annoyed with him for any reason. She hastened to reply that she was not, and continued, saying that something was changing in their relationship, that she couldn't understand her own behaviour. "Are you implying that we should stop seeing each other?" asked Lorenzo.

"No, never. God forbid any such thing to happen to our relationship," replied Catherine. "I think I am undergoing a change of sorts within me that makes me behave the way I do at times. I do feel uncomfortable when I see you, my heartbeat starts racing, I get nervous, find it difficult to keep my composure and feel shy. Please bear with me till I overcome this sudden change in me. I am too shy to take advice from anybody since this is a very personal matter between you and me. We have to be very patient and supportive of each other to overcome all by ourselves this new phase of our life. And triumph we will," she said, bowing her head down all along while she spoke. "Are you with me?" she asked Lorenzo.

"I will be with you till eternity," replied Lorenzo. Catherine heaved a sigh of relief.

Belinda and Antonio, who were watching them from the library window, were glad that they left Lorenzo and Catherine alone, fully satisfied with the outcome. They hurried back and joined them. Later that evening when the Jolly Foursome travelled back home, Lorenzo and Catherine sat together, saying nothing, but stealing a glance at each other repeatedly. They seemed to be comfortable when left alone. They longed for privacy and companionship, to express their feelings and emotions, to understand each other better now that they are grown up.

*

The next day, Belinda, Lorenzo's sister, left the house early to visit Catherine's residence. Catherine, who was leaning on the house veranda and daydreaming, woke up from her fantasy world when Belinda called her to greet her good morning. Surprised by the early bird's call, Catherine could not hide her embarrassment. "I called you three times when I approached your residence but you did not respond. What is happening? Are you alright? Is something bothering you? You can always confide in me," assured Belinda. Still reeling under the pressure of embarrassment, Catherine could not utter a word.

She collected her nerves together and forced a smile to greet Belinda good morning.

"Catherine, please tell me what's bothering you. I never saw you in this condition before. You keep to yourself and hardly talk these days. Maybe I can be of help to you. Don't you trust me? You know how much we all love and care about you. How much you mean to us all. Oh God we are going to be late for our lectures. Are you not going to attend classes today?"

"Yes I will, please wait for me Belinda. I will be ready in no time."

Both walked in silence together to board the bus, leaving Lorenzo and Antonio behind. When they reached the campus Belinda remembered that the professor would not be in for the first two lectures. "Let's find a place to sit and talk," suggested Belinda.

Catherine nodded in approval and said, "This is the right place to be, it is so peaceful."

Belinda heaved a sigh of relief on hearing Catherine speak at last. When they settled down on the campus grass, surrounded by trees all around them, Catherine thought to take advantage of the absence of Belinda's brothers, in whose presence she would not be able to talk about her dilemma.

Catherine spoke. "I do not understand what is wrong with me. I do feel nervous and uncomfortable when I see Lorenzo, my heartbeat starts racing, I get nervous, find it difficult to keep my composure or breathe, feel shy, and at times I sweat. I try hard to be normal but I just can't. It all started after the funeral when I hugged Lorenzo to offer my sympathies after most of the crowd left. While doing so I could not stop crying no matter how hard I tried. Sorrow and grief got the better of me. I kissed Lorenzo all over his face and held him tight for how long I know not.

"I came to my senses only when my emotionality subsided and realised what I did. I drew back, looked at him and ran as fast as I could, not to my residence but to Lorenzo's, to my surprise. Why, I do not know. Since that day my behaviour has changed towards him. I do not know what sort of opinion he has of me now. I hope against hope that he may not be mad at me. What I did was spontaneous in an emotionally charged atmosphere.

"It was not pre-planned. It just happened. I hope you believe me. I hope you understand. Please don't be mad at me. I want to apologise to Lorenzo and try to normalise my relationship with him. Till then I will not have peace of mind. Hope I can master courage to set things right between us. Belinda, you and your family have been best friends for generations together, and I desire that it stays that way for many more generations to come. I know lately my behaviour has changed drastically and you all worry about me, and so does my family."

Belinda moved closer to Catherine and held her hand. She drew back the hair from Catherine's face, wiped her tears and kissed her on her cheeks. Belinda spoke after a short pause, gathering her thoughts together to comfort her best childhood friend. "What happened at the funeral between you and Lorenzo was something very beautiful," remarked Belinda, and continued. "It was bound to happen sooner or later. Suppressed emotions give rise to sudden outburst without warning. They manifest the true feelings and emotions of a person. Such things do happen when two hearts beat for each other, always dreaming, thinking and longing to be with your love.

"Problems arise when these feelings are not expressed in a normal way may be due to fear or shyness, social restrictions, etc. With the passage of time these feelings, if not expressed, build up tension within and spill over in an uncontrolled manner. That's what happened to you, I feel, at the funeral. That is something natural for any human being to experience. You gave vent to your innermost feelings for Lorenzo which you had bottled up all these years. A sorrow-filled, charged atmosphere at the funeral brought forth your true feelings of love and compassion to Lorenzo and his family. My brother Lorenzo will certainly know for sure how much you love him. Be calm and stress-free. Think of the wonderful life that awaits you. Be sure and certain of it. My brother Lorenzo loves you dearly. By the way Catherine, what was my brother's reaction to you at the funeral?"

"Well when I hugged and kissed him I was crying. My eyes were full of tears. I rested my head on Lorenzo's chest and could not stop crying. He slowly held me in his arms. I felt he could not understand how to react or what to say. He stood in silence. When I withdrew from his arms I could feel his breath on my face. We kept looking at each other for a while. I can't forget that look of him. For me it seemed that he wanted to say something but could not.

"I keep thinking what it is that he wanted to say to me. Maybe he wanted me to stay with him to comfort him or just be there for him. He must have felt abandoned by me at a time and situation when he most needed me. How could I do such a thing to the one I love? Belinda you got to help me."

"I certainly will," assured Belinda. "What are friends for? I will catch him in his best of moods and raise the topic for discussion. Please, do not worry about anything. Time heals all wounds. We do not even know in what turmoil his heart and mind is at this moment. What he must be going through. I am sure he too has the same apprehension as you do."

*

That night Belinda could not sleep at all. She spent the whole night thinking of her brother Lorenzo. The night seemed extraordinarily long. Next day being Sunday, everybody visited church. Belinda teaches catechism for youngsters at the church after mass and Catherine plays piano for the church choir. Both are members of the church choir group. As Catherine left the church after they were done with their Sunday obligation, Catherine saw Lorenzo walking towards them in the opposite direction. Catherine held Belinda's hand. Her heart stopped beating; she stood still, as if mummified. She could not utter a word. Belinda comforted her not to worry. As Lorenzo approached them, they asked him whether he was looking for them. He replied in the negative. "I am here to give month's mind mass for our father."

Belinda replied that she had already done so, and now she had to visit the old age home. "Mr Braganza, who was supposed to visit the old age home today, is sick with fever. Bye, I'll catch up with you later."

Catherine was at her wits' end. Her lips and hands started shivering. Lorenzo realised he had to do something before she burst out crying. He moved towards Catherine, caught her hand in his, and kissed it. Catherine's eyes, still full of tears, struggled to see Lorenzo's face clearly. He reached for his handkerchief, still holding her hand, and wiped her tears.

Lorenzo: Catherine are you OK?

Catherine: Yes, I think so.

Lorenzo: Shall I bring you something to eat or drink? It may make you feel better.

Catherine: No. I will have breakfast at home.

Lorenzo: Why don't you join me for breakfast at my home? Please do not refuse.

Catherine: OK, but I may not be able to talk. I am very nervous already.

Lorenzo: Do I or my presence make you feel nervous? Don't we know each other since childhood?

Catherine: Yes, but now we are grown up.

Lorenzo: It is a natural process. We can't stop growing up.

Catherine: I get very nervous when I see you.

Lorenzo: Why?

Catherine: I do not know… or should I say, I know

but am afraid to talk about it.

Lorenzo: You will feel a whole lot better if you talk about it instead of suppressing it. And the sooner you do the better you will feel about yourself. The plight you are in now will just disappear. Can we meet at any place of your choice and talk? I feel we should meet very often to strengthen our relationship. That will clear many matters that are hindering the progress of our friendship. Shall I call for a taxi?

Catherine: No, please don't, I'll walk home with you.

Lorenzo: Are you sure?

Catherine: Yes I am.

Lorenzo: That is very encouraging.

Catherine: I feel a lot better talking to you.

Lorenzo: Me too. It is the right thing to do. Dialogue is essential in a relationship.

Catherine: I am very happy about today's developments.

Lorenzo: The sweet smile on your face says it all. I will see you tomorrow.

Lorenzo: Bye my love.

Catherine: Bye my sweetheart.

CHAPTER 4

Oh my love,
In you my soul delights
Your smile
Fresh morning dew
Fortunate to have only a few.

Belinda returned home from her visit to the old age home at half past noon. Lorenzo was not at home. It was unusual of him to stay out for so long. She wondered what was holding him up. He was always so very punctual. Then she remembered leaving Catherine with Lorenzo when she hurried to the old age home, and decided to visit Catherine. Stefano, Catherine's father, answered the door. After greeting Mr Stefano Pelagio, Belinda called out for Catherine. Mr Stefano told Belinda that she was still not in.

Surprised on hearing Stefano, Belinda requested Stefano to please tell Catherine to call her as soon as she returned, as she was a bit worried. Belinda decided to wait and see for a while if they were going to turn up, and if not, to go in search of them. She kept pacing in the veranda, restless and worried.

Just then, Lorenzo walked in. "What took you so

long?" asked Belinda. "Don't you know that we will be upset? What about Catherine? I left her with you, where is she?"

Just then Catherine walked in, smiling, and Belinda was relieved to see her.

*

As promised to Lorenzo, Catherine went to meet him after their lectures were done for the day. Lorenzo was all smiles to see Catherine. Seeing Lorenzo, she advanced towards him to meet him. She continued smiling and so did Lorenzo. This was their first date.

Catherine wore the beautiful traditional island costume – a striped woollen skirt worn with a red embroidered waistcoat, beautiful pleated blouse, shoulder scarf, and boots. Catherine is of medium height, and very pretty, with smooth fair skin, thick black hair, black eyes, and black eyebrows. Lorenzo wore the sash with a white linen shirt and baggy, knee-length trousers and *botachas* (boots). He too is fair-skinned and very handsome, with black hair, black eyes, and black eyebrows, medium height with a muscular build.

*

Catherine: Hello Lorenzo, so happy to see you.

Lorenzo: I am glad you came. You look very beautiful in the traditional Madeira outfit.

Catherine: I love to wear it. You too are dressed in a traditional Madeira outfit. It really suits you well.

Lorenzo: Thanks for the compliment. It's surprising to note that we think alike even though we did not plan to wear the traditional Madeira outfits.

Catherine: Yes, it surprised me too. I think it is a good sign to begin our first date, minds and hearts alike.

Lorenzo: Surely it is, and we should be happy.

*

Lorenzo presented her a beautiful bouquet of flowers comprising of Magnolia, Hottentot Fig, Hibiscus syriacus, Parrot Beak Lady's Slipper Orchids, Camellia, Broom Flowers, and the Bird-of-Paradise flower, which pleased Catherine so much that she embraced Lorenzo and kissed him passionately. Holding Catherine's hand, Lorenzo guided her steps in the direction of the jetty to board the ferry boat. They were escorted by the crew to their seats.

*

Catherine: I thought we were meeting at the college campus. This is a great surprise. This is a very romantic and beautiful place. I have never been here before. I am so happy, so thrilled to be here with you. I am glad you brought me here. You are very thoughtful, that is one of your qualities I admire. I don't know how many more are there to be discovered. What I did not know, was that you can be so romantic at times if you want to. I am very happy to know this side of your character. From today onwards I will have to reshape my thinking about you. I love you from the core of my humanity. I can't think of my life without you. I just can't.

Lorenzo: Neither can I. I am delighted to see you in a relaxed, happy mood.

Catherine: I think it's time for us to be optimistic about our career and future.

Moving a bit closer to Lorenzo, she held his hands in hers and kissed them.

Catherine: I feel that I am overcoming my nervousness and fears. The more time we spend together the more relaxed I feel. Currently, what I went through is something I could not understand myself, especially my behaviour. I feel losing your dad the way he died was a great shock for me. I could not accept the fact that he is no more. After the funeral when I approached you to offer my condolences, all my emotions and feelings spilled over, I kissed and hugged you for how long I know not. Then you enveloped me in your protective arms as I continued weeping bitterly on your shoulders. Suddenly when I came to my senses, I panicked and ran to your house instead of mine. I could not face you. I was too embarrassed and shy. Several thoughts crowded my mind. I could not think logically. It's then that I approached your sister Belinda for help. The rest is history.

The ferryboat captain blew the horn to announce the departure of the boat. The cruise delighted Catherine with eye-catching scenery, clear blue waters with white clouds hovering over them; sightings of dolphins delighted all, young and old, especially for the two young hearts, beating with the rhythm of love, savouring each moment of time spent on this cruise to treasure it for the rest of their lives. At times they said nothing, deeply engrossed in their thoughts, and yet they communicated much more than words can say. They expressed their feelings for each other in whispers, to be heard only by them, mindful of the presence of passengers, smiling as they whispered. They wanted no others in their midst, just the two of them, happy and content, being together.

How fast time flies, it waits for none. The cruise came to an end. It was time for them to return to their daily routine, but with a difference, the difference being accomplishing what they set out to do, to express their deep love for each other and a firm commitment to see it's fulfilment in their lives. As they stopped to part ways to go home, Catherine thanked Lorenzo for a very memorable outing for the first in her life. They embraced and kissed passionately. "From this day onwards I dedicate my life to you, my beloved," said Catherine, rolling her hand through Lorenzo's hair.

"And so do," I responded Lorenzo, holding her cheeks in both hands and planting a tender kiss on Catherine's lips. They locked in embrace, kissing and caressing, wishing and hoping for this moment to last forever. "Catherine my love, bye for now, till we meet again tomorrow."

"Bye my love Lorenzo, see you tomorrow."

Totally satisfied with the outcome of their cruise trip, they went home happy, weaving sweet dreams of the future that lay ahead of them.

Belinda saw from a distance the lovebirds hurrying home, holding hands with joy lit bright on their faces. Belinda ducked inside the house to hide from them, exhibiting total innocence on her face after witnessing their puppy love scene while they were marching home wholly engrossed in their love world. Antonio, who saw Belinda, his sister, hurriedly entering the house and smiling, wondered what mischief she was up to this time. When Antonio peeked from the house window to see his brother Lorenzo and Catherine walking hand in hand, he understood the strange behaviour of Belinda.

"Isn't it unbelievable to see our elder brother Lorenzo walking hand in hand with his childhood love Catherine? I just can't believe what I saw," remarked Antonio. "Isn't he the same shy, reserved boy of our village?" commented Antonio. "How come he mustered such courage and changed into a bold, matured individual instantly?"

Belinda said, "It is the power of the true, sincere, and pure love of Catherine and Lorenzo that emboldens them to overcome all hurdles of shyness and local customs to announce by their actions to the whole world that they are in love, and are fully equipped with determination to face the challenges that they may encounter."

The college term ended on a good note for Lorenzo, Antonio, Belinda, and Catherine too, as they all successfully moved into the second year of their studies after passing with good grades. It was time to relax and enjoy the holidays before college began.

Lorenzo decided to make good use of the holidays by devoting more time and attention to the boat building yard and fishing business. While attending college lectures he had to rely on his employees since he could put in only few hours of work in the afternoon after college. Antonio, Belinda, and Catherine extended their full support to Lorenzo in his quest to carry forward the family business of boat building and fishing to fulfil the promise he made to his father before he expired. The Jolly Foursome were back in action as a team once again.

∗

The next day Lorenzo left home early morning alone to his favourite spot. Catherine joined Antonio and Belinda at Lorenzo's residence. Catherine called for him but he wasn't at home. Belinda thought that Lorenzo was with Catherine at her residence. Puzzled, they looked at each other in disbelief, not knowing where Lorenzo could have gone so early in the morning. They sat wondering where to look for him. He was supposed to meet them at half past eight in the morning. Just then, Catherine stood up and asked Antonio and Belinda to follow her as she started running as fast as she could, followed by Antonio and Belinda.

They arrived at the Camaro de Lobos beach and found him sitting at the edge of the beach, staring at the blue sea. Totally exhausted, they dropped onto the beach gasping for breath, Catherine leaning on Lorenzo's back with arms round his neck. "We looked for you at home. Then I knew where to find you."

Lorenzo visits this spot often for relaxation and inspiration when he has to make important decisions. He loves the scenic beauty of this place, clear blue sea water, waves dashing on the rocks splashing showers on people passing by, small crabs burrowing in the sand with incredible speed, fishermen pulling their nets ashore with their catch, seagulls flying and occasionally snatching a fish, lovers walking hand in hand.

After recovering from the exhaustion they settled down to begin their meeting to chart out the programme for the vacation. "So far, since my father's death to date we fared well in business," commented Lorenzo. "It's a very encouraging sign for us all. I would like to take this opportunity to thank and congratulate the Jolly Foursome for doing well as a team by surpassing the set target beyond our imagination. You will be rewarded generously.

"I would like to place before the team members (the core group) Antonio, Belinda, and Catherine, the future plan of action I have drafted for the next ten years. I request each member of the team to take a copy and study the proposed plan of action. Your views and suggestions would be highly appreciated. I am encouraged by your dedication and support to move forward with renewed zeal and determination. We will discuss the plan after I get feedback from all the team members and key management personnel.

"I would like to thank my loving brother Antonio, sister Belinda, loyal friend Catherine, and her parents, and not forgetting the key management personnel and technical experts who contributed immensely in guiding and advising on very important issues for achieving total success in this project. We will meet again as soon as we are ready to deliberate on the project. The plan that I have drafted is an outline of the final plan that will emerge after we discuss in detail all aspects of the plan. A unanimous decision will be taken by the core group and key management personnel in confidence. We will move forward only when we have a unanimous decision from the core group. As we proceed with the project we will have to evaluate the feasibility of the project and incorporate necessary changes as and when deemed necessary. It is a continuous process. Thank you for attending the meeting. Let's chill out and have fun, for we are on vacation with a mission."

CHAPTER 5

To tap the inborn talent
One must be conscious of the natural gift.
Channelling all resources for its fulfilment
Brings forth rewards mighty and swift.
Courage my Son don't fear or drift
Accomplish you will with vision and lift.

All core group members, the key management personnel and technical experts of the A. J. Rebeiro Yard approved the proposal with a thumping majority. Lorenzo was delighted for their support and encouragement. All admired him for his vision and foresight. His project was unique in the sense that he incorporated fair business practices, human development programs, and conservation of nature.

❖ Expanding the boat building yard with the available technology in a planned manner to keep pace with the ever-increasing market demand.
❖ Training and motivating the workforce to maximise production.

❖ Starting a new venture to market fish products for export and local consumption.

❖ Manufacturing of quality nets on a commercial scale for export and local use.

❖ The management has offered free repairs and maintenance to the traditional fishermen.

❖ Opening up centres to preserve traditional arts and craft vocations to generate employment.

*

To practice what he preached, he modernised his boat building yard with the available technology during that period which conserved nature, and enhanced human productivity and development. To improve the lot of the traditional fisherman, Lorenzo forwarded a proposal to the government department concerned to provide motors, nets, and fuel at a subsidised rate to lessen the hardships of the traditional fisherman to run their trade profitably.

By fitting motors to their traditional fishing boats they will not have to labour hard to row the boat against the vagaries of nature like storms. They will save time which they can use to relax, mend their nets, and spend quality time with their families. The quality of life they will enjoy will enhance their longevity and productivity. Lorenzo has also assured the traditional fisherman that he will do free-of-charge repairs and maintenance for those who are struggling for survival with their trade, and provide nets.

Lorenzo started a recreational facility for people of all ages and genders to channel their energies in a productive way and be safe. He opened a marine institute and employed retired fishermen to pass on the skills and expertise to the younger generation, who can be employed in the marine trade industry. He established a football club to tap the talent of the youth and organised tournaments. For the fair sex, he established centres for learning embroidery, tailoring, etc., and established scholarships for economically backward classes.

Lorenzo was to head the management team, followed by his brother Antonio as Business Administrator for the approved plan, Catherine as Director of Finance, Trade and Commerce, and Belinda as Personnel Manager and Marketing Executive. All were pleased with the outcome and very eager to resume their new roles to gain valuable work experience, besides completing their studies. Catherine and Lorenzo's family were very happy the way things were taking shape. Catherine admired Lorenzo, but now she adored him for his business acumen and foresightedness.

*

Lorenzo shed away his shyness as days passed by, since he was seeing Catherine very often. They loved to spend time together. Catherine enjoyed the last cruise trip and suggested to Lorenzo they go on another one, in a quiet but beautiful surrounding like the Jardine Botanico. Lorenzo immediately accepted her suggestion and planned a trip before their vacation ends and college begins the new term.

On their arrival at the Jardine Botanico they were totally amazed with the beautiful sight that welcomed them. They liked it so much they danced for joy. They spent the whole day fully engrossed among themselves in the beautiful romantic surroundings. "We will cherish these beautiful moments, especially the memorable time we spent together for the rest of our life, won't we?" asked Catherine, to which Lorenzo replied, "Surely we will."

*

Brother Antonio, sister Belinda, and mother Isabela were fully satisfied with Lorenzo's vision and leadership. "It runs in the family blood," commented Isabela, mother of Lorenzo, holding his cheeks in her hands and kissing him.

Lorenzo knows very well that he has a great responsibility ahead of him to succeed in his business venture. He has to his advantage, since his very childhood, all the necessary skill, confidence and experience needed to succeed in the trade. He is studying to qualify to be a Marine Engineer – that will boost his confidence further. Stefano Pelagio, who is a wealthy man himself, is very happy with the way Lorenzo is progressing with his business and life.

Catherine's nights are restless. She constantly dreams of Lorenzo till she falls asleep to wake up before dawn, lying in bed lazily till the first glimmer of light appears, to see first the face of her beloved Lorenzo before anyone else's, to shower on him flying kisses by leaning on the house balcony opposite Lorenzo's. She repeats this routine every morning and Lorenzo makes sure he is available to receive the shower of kisses every morning.

Belinda's aggressive marketing strategy paid rich dividends as she hauled in enough orders to keep the workforce busy for the next four years. She surprised herself and the management by achieving this great feat beyond her expectations. She cried with tears of joy and vowed to do even better in memory of her loving father, who was a great achiever. Lorenzo's family celebrated Belinda's success at their residence, accompanied by Catherine and Stefano Pelagio. All employees were happy with Belinda's success as their future would be safe if business progressed. Belinda's success brought in the much-needed popularity for A. J. Rebeiro Boat Building Yard.

Catherine and Belinda bonded well in their friendship. Those who do not know them well, think they are sisters. Those who know them envy their friendship. They are inseparable. They are always together no matter where they are. They care about each other and their friendship. They share everything that goes on in their lives. But today Belinda is quiet; Catherine did most of the talking and noticed that Belinda was lost in her own world. Catherine shook Belinda to bring her back to her senses. "Belinda, you seemed lost in your own world. What is bothering you? You can always confide in me."

"That's what I am going to do right now. You know my cousin's brother Romeo, don't you?"

"Yes I do, is he alright?" queried Catherine.

"He is fine. I received a letter from him today delivered by his friend Ronaldo while I was returning home from the market. This letter is addressed to my brother Lorenzo and I don't know whether I have done the right thing by accepting the letter. Suddenly Ronaldo appeared in front of me from nowhere and said, 'This is for you,' handed the letter to me, and disappeared as swiftly as he came, giving me no time to react or think. I am living in fear lest anybody should come to know about it. I will be in great trouble. You know what the reason is?"

"Yes I do," confirmed Catherine. "There is no need to panic. We have to think over this matter carefully and with a cool mind. Do not worry, we will find a way to settle this matter. Did you open the letter, Belinda?"

"No I didn't. I am too afraid to open the letter," replied Belinda.

"How will you know what is written in the letter? I think you should read the letter. Do not fear, fear is an illusion, but reason is wisdom," commented Catherine. "All your fear and anxiety will vanish in a moment once you read the letter."

There was a deep rift between Belinda's ancestors and that of Romeo's over a disputed land claimed by both the families to be theirs. This dispute legacy had been passed on for generations. Neither family's elders made any effort to settle this matter peacefully, instead they stuck to their demands, stubborn as ever. They lived with false pride and passed away, leaving a legacy of animosity and hatred to the surviving generations. Even when the younger generation tried to reconcile and live in peace with each other the elders frustrated their efforts, such was the hatred among these two families with the same bloodline. Belinda's family decided to give up their rights over the disputed property so that both families could leave in peace. Romeo's family sold the property and their ancestral house and moved to Machico and settled there.

CHAPTER 6

Death is a reality there is no escape
When where or how no one can say.
Take comfort in the promise of eternal life
Nothing else can erase the strife.

Romeo's parents, Matilda and Jerome, died in a car accident. Romeo, being the only son of Matilda and Jerome, is orphaned by the death of his parents with no contact with the rest of the family spread over the island. The only family he remembers is Belinda's. He still has fond memories of his youthful days when he spent his whole school holidays with his cousins Lorenzo, Belinda, and Antonio. He never turned down an invitation to visit his cousins since his cousins, too, were very fond of him.

Three months has passed by since the death of his parents and Romeo cannot decide whether he should inform his cousins or not. He has had no contact with them for the last twelve years because of the strained relation between the elders. He is not sure what sort of a welcome awaits him. He still has, fresh in his memory, the ugly scenes he witnessed as a youngster between his dad and his uncle.

Both families never allowed their children to get involved in the conflict. It was always the elders of the two families. Romeo, a qualified architect himself, took over the family business. Jerome's last words to his son were: "Reconcile with your Uncle Alberto Joao Ribeiro's family, and do not follow in my footsteps." To respect his dad's last wish he decided to write to his uncle's family about the death of his parents. And this is the letter which Belinda received from Romeo, sent with his friend to personally deliver it to his uncle's family.

Dear Cousin Lorenzo,

Pardon me for writing to you after a gap of twelve long years. It was my mum and dad's last wish that I reconcile with my Uncle Alberto Joao Ribeiro's family and not to follow in my parents footsteps. My mum and dad died of a car accident three months back. I find it very difficult to cope up with my life without them. There was so much to do after their death. My friends and our employees were of great help. My life is in turmoil. How soon three months elapsed, I do not know. I am just beginning to pull myself together from this great loss and trying to live a normal life. It is not easy though. I have to accept the reality of my life and carry on. I am not sure how you will react to this news given the past history of our families. And that is the reason why I delayed in informing you.

Your cousin
Romeo Jerome Ribeiro

Catherine took the letter from Belinda and examined it carefully, and realised that the letter was addressed to Lorenzo. Catherine suggested to Belinda to hand over the letter to Lorenzo since it was addressed to him. Belinda found Catherine's suggestion logical and decided to act upon it. They both marched home to hand over the letter to Lorenzo, who was deeply engrossed in his work. "I would be so happy if you would spare some thought for me and get deeply engrossed in me the way you do with your work," commented Catherine.

Hearing this, Lorenzo felt shy and embarrassed of his sister's presence and smiled, saying, "Belinda do not pay attention to what she says. I will get engrossed in her after we are married, but now I have to concentrate on my work. There is so much to be done. I would appreciate if all of us would get engrossed in our work responsibilities with love and total dedication. I am fully satisfied so far with your performance and total support, and I truly appreciate it. All I say is, do not be satisfied with what we have already achieved – there is lot to conquer."

"We came to see you to hand over this letter to you delivered by your cousin Romeo through his friend Ronaldo."

"Oh, what a pleasant surprise!" exclaimed Lorenzo. "We have not heard from him for so long. At last he wrote to us. I am so excited to read the letter. I can't wait. Hope everything goes back to our childhood days, happy days. I am sure Romeo has good news of a family reunion. How much I long to believe it to be true. How nice it would be to recount our childhood memories, live in peace and harmony for the rest of our lives. I am very optimistic that something is going to change our lives for a better tomorrow."

Excitedly, Lorenzo opened the letter to read. Lorenzo could not believe what he read. He was in a great shock. He sank into the sofa, his hands shivering, tears rolling from his eyes. Catherine and Belinda could not understand why he was suddenly crying so much. Lorenzo could not say anything, such was the grief that he had to use sign language to communicate with them. Catherine and Belinda tried to calm him down but to no success.

Belinda took the letter from his hand and on reading, realised the gravity of the problem. Belinda rushed into the house to break the news to her mother. The crying and wailing became louder; that attracted the attention of their neighbours. Mr Pelagio rushed to Lorenzo's house in response to the commotion and was shocked to hear the sad news. Soon the whole neighbourhood assembled at Lorenzo's residence offering condolences and praying for the dead souls. As news spread of the tragedy a sea of people came to offer their heartfelt sympathies and prayers.

Nobody was prepared to face such an eventuality. It took everyone by surprise. Lorenzo's family was totally grief-stricken. People came to offer condolences, comfort, and moral support to share their grief. They never expected death to be so cruel, so brutal, that it left them speechless and disoriented. The words of comfort sounded too hollow to be realistic. They refused to be consoled. Neither could they run away from the reality that was before them. Both families were in deep sorrow. Isabela remembered constantly her orphaned nephew Romeo. She was wondering how Romeo must have felt, cooped up with his sorrow all alone. She felt duty bound to be with her nephew. The next day Lorenzo's family, together with Stefano Pelagio's family, left to Machico to meet Romeo Jerome Ribeiro.

All of them were lost in their thoughts about the happenings, perhaps in introspection, searching for answers. Isabela thought of Romeo the whole journey, wondering what he must have felt on hearing the news. How he must have coped with the loss of both parents snatched away by fate in an instant. Not a single relative present to help or comfort him. Facing the past rivalry barrier to contact them must have torn him apart; distressed, abandoned, being forsaken by those he loved all his life must have totally devastated him.

The vehicle they were travelling in came to a halt that awakened them from their deep thoughts. Romeo stood at the entrance to invite them in. All expressed their grief and sorrow to Romeo, hugging, kissing and consoling him all the time. The visitors tried their level best to hold back their tears when they visited the cemetery but could not do so as they were just beginning to realise the gravity of the tragedy that took away two lives. The visitors assured Romeo of a new beginning by leaving the past behind. They apologised for their past mistakes. Romeo accepted their apologies and thanked them. Isabela and Belinda stayed behind at Romeo's residence to help Romeo settle down to lead a normal life. Two weeks later Isabela and Belinda returned to their residence assuring Romeo of personal attention and continuous support and help.

CHAPTER 7

Leaving the past behind
Keeping the future in mind.
March forward a purpose to find
The meaning of life.
And when you find one
You will never look behind.

Romeo decided to move on with his life by drowning himself in his architecture profession, leaving early, returning home late, totally drained of all energy. Live for work, work for life seemed to be his motto. He was going through a totally different phase in his life, a life of loneliness, and could not understand how to react to it. He was now lonely in this wild world. Life seemed empty, meaningless with no one to comfort, to advise, to love, to keep company. Everyone seemed too busy to spare a thought for someone in need. All were rushing to meet deadlines to cope with life's demand, to excel better than the others, to achieve targets, to outsmart their competitors.

Romeo is one of the architects who succeeded in his profession at a very young age and carved out a distinguished reputation in his career to be the best, envy of many, and prosperous. In spite of all his achievements he led a simple life, but wasn't happy. He could feel that there was something missing in his life but could not decide what it was. His relatives made a point to visit him once every week to keep him company and to strengthen the family bond. But that didn't help in his quest to find out what he really wanted. Family bonds are important and necessary, and Romeo had them in abundance, especially after the demise of his parents in a car accident.

He tries day in and day out to try and figure out what it is that is bothering him so much that he cannot guess or recollect. He tries to keep himself busy with social work, hobbies like gardening which he loves so much, visiting age old homes and providing for their needs, helping needy students by funding their studies to gain skills to better their future prospects; kind-hearted, generous, no wonder he is very popular among the masses.

Returning home one day after a very tiring day, Romeo freshened himself and settled down with a glass of wine. He picked up the newspaper to read. As he turned the pages, a photograph caught his attention. He observed the photograph closely but wasn't sure who it may be. By sheer instinct, unconsciously, he kept the whole newspaper in his personal drawer and settled down to sip the wine, have dinner, and retire for the night. Sleep evaded him no matter how hard he tried to sleep – he kept thinking of the photograph he saw in the newspaper. He gave up trying to sleep only to realise in the morning he had slept like a log. He had no knowledge of when he dozed off.

Next morning he got ready to leave for his daily work routine. As he was leaving, the phone rang. He wondered who could be calling him at this time in the morning. He rushed back in the house to answer the call, picked up the receiver and said, "Hello, who is calling?"

A sweet voice, yes, a sweet voice greeted him, inquiring whether it was the residence of Romeo Jerome Ribeiro. Surprised to hear a lady's voice, he paused for a moment, not knowing what to say. He got his nerves together and answered in a nervous tone, "Yes it's my residence. Who is calling?"

"It's me, I mean, Susanna Saldana. Does this name sounds familiar to you?"

"I am confused, I can't recollect," replied Romeo. "I will think over it and get in touch with you if I remember."

"I will eagerly wait for your call Romeo, please do call," pleaded Susanna.

"I promise, I will," Romeo assured his unknown admirer.

Romeo lost his peace of mind with this strange lady's call. On his journey to the office he kept wondering who she could be. *She knows my name and residence telephone number. How did she get my personal details? I don't remember knowing any lady by that name. Maybe I know her but can't recollect her now.* Romeo now regretted not noting down her landline number to contact her. *How silly of me. Now I have no hope to contact her. Hope she calls back soon and puts an end to this suspense. It's bothering me too much and takes my concentration away from my life's daily routine.*

*

Sitting close to the telephone at her family residence, Susanna anxiously waits for the call from Romeo. She is restless, not knowing why the call isn't coming. Every minute that ticks by makes her lose hope but she keeps comforting herself not to give up, but to persevere in hope. Little did she know what was causing the delay, and that Romeo was helpless to contact her, not having telephone number. Susanna is very upset and desperate to get in touch with Romeo.

Susanna's father, Ronaldo Saldana, had purchased a house with a mortgage but could not pay the same due to financial difficulties since he lost all his business investments. Now he has to vacate the property for failing to pay the mortgage. He has only one month's time to do so; either pay or leave.

No sooner had Romeo entered his office, the phone rang. Impatiently, Susanna asked for Romeo. "Yes, it's Romeo with you."

"Thank God you answered. Sorry to bother you. It's me again, Susanna. I have been desperately trying to get in touch with you as I need your help urgently. Please help us. Please do not refuse. Only you can save us from this situation."

Romeo was alarmed to hear what he heard. He tried to calm her down, assuring her of his help. She sounded nervous and frightened while giving residence details to Romeo. He noted down the details and requested Susanna to stay at home as he was on his way to see her at her residence.

CHAPTER 8

Reunion makes happy ending,
Tears of joy heralds home coming,
Emotions over rides all barriers,
Past is forgotten future seems merrier.

On reaching Susanna's residence, he was surprised to see a familiar face, but wasn't sure of it. Susanna on the other hand was totally shocked to see Romeo, whom she recognised instantly, but could not believe what she saw. "Am I dreaming or is it real? After all these years I had given up all hopes of a reunion," she murmured.

Susanna and Romeo fixed their gaze on each other as if they were hypnotised. Susanna motioned towards Romeo with tears rolling down her cheeks, believing in the impossible happenings. She stopped in front of Romeo, embracing him and crying her heart out with joy and Romeo responded to the unfolding developments by enveloping Susanna in his arms. For a moment they got lost with their feelings of joy. Susanna escorted Romeo to her residence, still holding Romeo in her comforting arms. As they entered they were greeted by Ronaldo Saldana, father of Susanna. He was shocked but also happy to see Romeo and Susanna together once again.

Susanna and Romeo were the residents of the Azores in Madeira, Portugal. They grew up together till they completed their graduation. Then the unexpected happened. Fire engulfed the whole of Madeira, destroying everything – nothing was spared. Many people were not fortunate enough to escape the blazing fire; some died, some managed to swim for safety, others fled by boats and by whatever means they could to save their lives. Lives were shattered beyond hope of a future. In this chaotic situation many family members got scattered throughout the island. Romeo and Susanna, too, got separated and since they did not hear about each other, they gave up hope of a reunion, not knowing what fate they met.

Romeo was in mainland Portugal when this tragedy took place. He rushed back to Madeira as soon as normalcy was restored on Madeira. He marched straight to the residence of Susanna only to find the house completely destroyed, in ashes. He desperately tried to trace her whereabouts with no success.

And here they are together once again, unbelieving eyes exposing them to the stark reality of their life. They embraced firmly, caressing and kissing, not knowing what to say even though they had so much to say. Their eyes, lips, tears, and caressing hands did all the talking. They were content to at last have each other for themselves, to share their love and life. What a beautiful moment, how fortunate to be together when all hope was lost.

Fate, faithfulness, and true love coupled with total

dedication won them the victory against all odds. They were blessed when there was no hope of a blessing, united when in despair – that's how true love rewards faithfulness. For a moment they forgot all that they went through, the agonising pain of a separation, the uncertain future ahead of them, no hope of ever seeing or hearing any news of their whereabouts, no hope of filling the void that existed in their life, wanting so much to be united, never ever to be separated again. And their prayer was answered.

The call that Susanna made in desperation to Romeo turned out to be a great blessing for her and her family. The house that Ronaldo Saldana purchased with a mortgage happened to be that of Romeo Ribeiro Builders Ltd. Romeo had no knowledge of the sale to Ronaldo Saldana as he concentrated his full attention on negotiating property deals, architecture, and finance, while sales were taken care of by his sales team. When Romeo's attention was drawn by his sales team to the failure to pay mortgage dues for six months by Mr Ronaldo Saldana, he took immediate steps to investigate the matter and was surprised to learn that this particular property belonged to Mr Ronaldo Saldana and daughter Susanna.

Romeo cancelled the mortgage and issued an occupancy certificate to them. Ronaldo Saldana heaved a sigh of relief for his generosity and thanked Romeo for his help. Ronaldo Saldana sold his property that was gutted by fire to pay the balance on the mortgage amount to Romeo, which Romeo declined to accept.

Susanna, witnessing all the unfolding events, could

not contain her emotions, and left the place to be all by herself. Romeo took leave of Ronaldo Saldana, assuring him of his continuous patronage. Ronaldo Saldana felt comforted by his reassuring words and thanked Romeo.

That night, sleep evaded both of them. Night seemed extraordinarily lengthy. They had so much to say to each other, so much to ask and to listen to. They kept their minds occupied with romantic thoughts to express their innermost feelings at dawn. They kept rehearsing their lines lest they should forget with nervousness. Night gave way to a new dawn, a dawn they were awaiting expectantly to make a new beginning of a new life, totally different than the one they had lived so far. At times, mixed feelings dampened their joy, but reassuring thoughts restored their confidence to face life.

Susanna wondered, *What does this all mean? Cancellation of the mortgage and transferring the property documents to Ronaldo Saldana. He must have done this out of real concern for us, otherwise why he would refuse to accept payment from my dad? Does he love me still? Is he going to marry me? Oh, silly me to think of such a thing now that he is a very successful businessman; rich, famous, and popular among the masses. How will I find out what's on his mind? Better I wait patiently and watch the future development unfold,* concluded Susanna. *That seems to be a sensible thing to do. Yes, I will wait and watch.*

CHAPTER 9

Those who wait with hope and faith expectantly
Will surely receive what they hope for
Long is the night for him who cannot sleep.
Joy fills the heart with morning breeze.

At daybreak Romeo paced restlessly in his bedroom, lost in some thoughts of his own, perhaps trying to make up his mind concerning something important. After a great deal of thought Romeo made up his mind and called Susanna's residence. He was greeted by Susanna, who blushed on hearing Romeo's voice. There was a brief pause.

*

Romeo: Hello Susanna. It's me, Romeo.

Susanna: Yes I know, I am pleased with your call. Why did you call?

That question sent shivers down his spine and he forgot what he had rehearsed to say to Susanna. He tried in vain to recollect his thoughts but failed. He paused for a while, desperately trying to speak but could not. Susanna could hear him breathing heavily and sensed that maybe he was too nervous to say what he wanted to say.

Susanna: Are you with me Romeo? Why are you silent?

Romeo: Yes I am with you. I spent all night rehearsing what I will say to you but now my mind is blank and I am at a loss of words. It is very embarrassing.

Susanna: Maybe I can help you if you allow me to.

Romeo: I give up and accept your offer.

Susanna: You are in love, aren't you Romeo?

Romeo: Yes I am, but how do you know that I am in love with you?

Susanna: I didn't know till this moment. It's you who confessed your love for me just now. You love me, isn't that true?

Romeo: Yes it is, but I am too shy to express it. Now that you have helped me to express my true feelings I am relieved. Thanks for your help.

Susanna: You are most welcome. I am glad that I could be of help to you. Don't you think it will be wise for us to meet often? It will help you to overcome your shyness, build confidence and trust in us and feel more comfortable. Fate once again reunited us when there was nothing to hope for. I had given up all hopes of a reunion. Now we have a second chance to make the most of our life that is ahead of us, so let us get started.

Romeo: How did you cope with your life immediately after the tragedy struck Madeira? It must have been a nightmare for you and for the entire population living on Madeira.

Susanne: Yes, I was totally shattered to witness the tragedy unfold without warning. Fire engulfed the whole island. There was utter chaos and confusion as people moved in all directions to find an escape route. Mothers running for their lives with small children, trying to save them. I do not know whether they made it to safety or not. Families got scattered all over. There was death and destruction everywhere. Charred bodies strewn all over the island beyond recognition, houses were reduced to ashes. I managed to navigate to the shore of Madeira and sat on a rock close to the water, frightened, hungry, homeless, and exhausted with the ordeal I went through.

I sat there crying, thinking of the many unfortunate ones who could not make it to the shore. Then I saw a huge number of people gathered at the shore of Madeira. Many fishing boats approached the island jetty to rescue the stranded people. There was joy and sorrow, sadness and disappointments. The whole island was in mourning. I was the fortunate one to survive among many others. For the first time in my life I witnessed death so close to me, it's like being born again. If it wasn't for the fishermen, the death toll would have been much higher. They fought gallantly against the rough sea to rescue people without caring for their own safety. They were the real heroes. The whole of Madeira owes much to these gallant soldiers of the sea.

Romeo: Susanna, you are a brave woman and I admire you for your courage. Women are said to be blessed with inner strength which helps them to overcome difficult situations in life. That's what you did, with your instinct to save your life. I am proud of you.

Both remained silent for a while, perhaps to gather their thoughts together to continue with the conversation. Then both simultaneously broke the silence by saying, "You know…" then paused for a while. Romeo at last spoke.

Romeo: Susanna, please express your feelings freely. I am too eager to listen what you have to say.

Susanna: I already expressed my innermost feelings to you recently. But today I am feeling shy to do so.

Romeo: But why?

Susanna: I honestly do not know why. Please, I beg of you not to be mad at me. I stand by my word, I assure you.

Romeo: That's very comforting. But not comforting enough to have peace of mind.

Susanna: Oh Romeo I will never put you through that ordeal. I care about you more than words can say. I am at a loss of words to express my gratitude to you for being so kind and generous for helping us out from difficult circumstances. I promise my total love, faithfulness and dedication to you for the rest of my life.

Romeo: Oh Susanna, you are my life's precious possession. You are like romantic poetry written on my heart with your enchanting smile, your beauty, your gracefulness and caring attitude. I consider myself very fortunate to have you as my companion to share my life.

Susanna: That's fine with me, but we must plan our future together before we are married. That will help us to focus our attention on the plan instead of taking rash decisions which most of the time prove to be unproductive. We will have to revise the plan according to the circumstances of our life situation. Planning in advance will give us an added advantage as we will be well prepared to face unforeseen developments. Don't you think so Romeo?

Romeo: Yes, I agree with you. You do have wisdom and foresight. That's why I love and adore you so much. God has been too gracious to you to bless you with so much of wisdom and knowledge.

Susanna: We got so engrossed in our own world that we forgot to visit or even call Lorenzo and Catherine.

Romeo: Better we surprise them with a personal visit and catch up with the latest happenings.

Susanna: Yes, we will do just that.

CHAPTER 10

Doubts cloud the mind with obscurity,
Blinds a person with no clarity.
Clarity dispels misunderstanding of minds
Joy returns when peace is found.

Lorenzo's success caught the attention of all in the ship building industry, which made him very popular. His generosity is well known among the masses. Lorenzo did not let his success distract his attention or change his attitude or character. He remains focused at all times to accomplish his mission. He knows that he has a long way to go. This is just the beginning. His success boosted his morale and that of his team. He knows that he has to capitalise on his success to consolidate his position in the industry. He has to better his performance to be the very best in this industry. He has to be innovative and introduce new technology for the advancement of the industry and commerce.

As he was contemplating on this matter, suddenly the telephone rang. He sprang to his feet and rushed to answer the call. Lorenzo was speechless and in a rude shock. He could not believe what he heard. He totally went dumb and stood motionless as if hypnotised by a ghost. Confused by Lorenzo's behaviour, Catherine decided to leave without uttering a word, switch on her car and drive away. It was too late for Lorenzo to react. He could not understand how to handle the situation. He just sank in his chair and wondered what to do next. He remembered his best friend Francisco, called him, narrated him the situation and asked for his help.

Lorenzo got so engrossed in his work, like a workaholic, that he forgot everything including his sweetheart Catherine. Constant travel on business trips took a toll on their intimate relationship. Stefano Pelagio, who is a very successful businessman himself, knows well the feelings of his daughter Catherine and comforts her by narrating his real life experiences. Belinda and Antonio play their part well as best friends of Catherine to comfort and reassure her about their brother Lorenzo.

Stefano Pelagio comforts Catherine by saying that he finds nothing wrong with Lorenzo's behaviour. "Please do not draw conclusions about him without hearing him first. Highly ambitious and motivated people exhibit such behaviour very often. They remain fully focused to achieve their goals, so much so that nothing else matters till they succeed. Once they succeed they turn normal, being relieved from the stress, worries and risks they take to succeed. It's not easy to succeed in a competitive world. It takes courage, determination, confidence and lots of patience."

Catherine listened carefully to her father's advice and decided to act on it. Stefano Pelagio heaved a sigh of relief.

Francisco: Lorenzo do you have any knowledge of how long it has been that you last saw Catherine?

Lorenzo: No I don't, I guess it may be a month or two.

Francisco: Lorenzo, it has been three months as of today.

Lorenzo: Three months, are you sure Francisco?

Francisco: Yes I am, and not only I but all concerned who are affected by your behaviour.

Lorenzo: My behaviour, what is wrong with my behaviour?

Francisco: You have no time for your family – no calls, no contact. Everybody feels you are no longer the same caring person they once knew and that includes Catherine who loves you so much.

Lorenzo: Francisco I am too busy now. Please bear with me for another two weeks. I will be back home by then. As far as Catherine is concerned, I love her and all my family and specially you, Francisco. I understand you all feel neglected at the moment but that is not true. Take care, bye.

Lorenzo hurriedly calls Catherine and she answers immediately.

Catherine: Hello Lorenzo, I am so happy to hear your voice. To me it seems ages the last time I heard you. I am totally relieved to hear you. Please say something. Hope you are not angry with me. I love you and missed you so much, no words can express my feelings for you.

Lorenzo could not believe what he heard. He was expecting Catherine to burst out with anger for ignoring not only her but his family too. Instead he gets a warm, loving reception on the phone from Catherine. He remained speechless, not knowing what to say. He had rehearsed the explanation to give in his defence. But here, he hangs onto the phone, confused.

Catherine: Lorenzo are you there? Please speak.

Lorenzo: Yes Catherine, I am with you. I apologise for not keeping contact with you while I am away. I am still extremely busy with meetings, finalising deals, meeting people, educating myself about the latest technology, etc. I will be back soon. I did miss you all a lot, I really did. I am feeling homesick too.

Catherine: I know you are working tirelessly to make a success of your business plan and be where you want to be. You have full backing from all of us; you are not alone. I know my love that you missed me and all family members since this is the first time you had to stay away from home for so long. We are eagerly waiting for your safe return. Please come soon. My dad has full confidence in you, so much so that he advised me not to draw conclusions about you without hearing you first.

Honestly I was a mental wreck wondering what's holding you up from calling us for so long. I did get negative thoughts about you, but my dad's timely advice dispelled all my doubts and fears. Now I am at peace with myself and waiting eagerly to hug you on your arrival. I love you with all my heart.

Lorenzo, having succeeded in accomplishing his

mission overseas, decided to return home fully satisfied with his achievements, and called all his family and informed of his arrival. They all danced with joy and planned a warm reception for him.

The momentary sadness that they all experienced recently gave way to joy with smiles writ large on their faces. All family members participated to prepare a warm welcome for Lorenzo. On the day of his arrival all were present to welcome him, including Stefano Pelagio and Catherine, with a beautiful bouquet of flowers symbolising love. Lorenzo thanked them for such a warm welcome and expressed his joy to return home among his loved ones. They all visited the **Sao Sebastiao** church to participate in a mass which was offered by Lorenzo's mother for his success. The whole village of Camara de Lobos and the management core group turned up for the mass as they were warmly invited to participate, followed by a lavish banquet.

Catherine is too anxious to be with Lorenzo to spend some precious moments with him after a gap of three months. Stefano Pelagio observed Catherine's uneasiness and requested all present to let Lorenzo freshen up and take rest. As Lorenzo's family house was full of relatives who were staying for the night, Catherine suggested that he spend the night at her residence in peace and quiet to sleep and rest, to which all guests and relatives had a hearty laugh. Catherine blushed and ran to her residence, followed by Lorenzo. Stefano Pelagio welcomed him with a hug and a kiss. Catherine held Lorenzo's hand and led him to her room to be alone with him.

Catherine: Lorenzo I am sorry for not welcoming

you with a kiss and a hug as I would feel shy and embarrassed doing so in public, especially in front of our parents and all our relatives.

Lorenzo: Catherine, you did the right thing and I am truly impressed with your behaviour. That's why I love and adore you. You are a very sensitive individual, that's why I try to be very careful with my behaviour towards you so that I do not hurt your feelings in any way. Concerning my long absence for three months without calling anyone back home, I owe an apology to you and the rest of the family.

Catherine: Lorenzo please, there is no need to apologise. Nobody wants one from you. By offering one you may hurt their feelings and mine too. All of us have full confidence in you. We know your nature very well.

Lorenzo: Catherine but I still want to talk about it with you, if not with others.

Catherine: I trust you my love, and so does everyone else. Let us talk about us.

Lorenzo: Are you sure, Catherine?

Catherine: Absolutely sure. Lorenzo, it's I who has to apologise, not you.

Lorenzo: But why?

Catherine: I did doubt you for a moment, but not for long. But what would I do under such circumstances? I could not think rationally. I was a mental wreck passing sleepless nights. After all, you are a very successful businessman – handsome, rich, and famous. You do understand what I mean, don't you?

Lorenzo: Yes I do. Anybody in your place would have reacted the same way. After all, my behaviour was also very irrational towards everybody and I am fully responsible for my actions. It is true that I was extremely busy and was optimistic to complete my mission within a short period, but it didn't turn out as I expected. I did try to strictly stick to my schedule but could not do so as some things were beyond my control. I did book my appointments well in advance and they were confirmed by the concerned authorities but some of them had to be rescheduled as the other parties could not show up.

I had no other option but to resign to my situation, accept the new appointments, complete my mission and return back home. I like to stick to my deadlines. I was very upset and was not in a proper frame of mind. It took me sometime to pull myself together and complete my mission. In the end I was happy as I was able to achieve what I set to achieve and returned home fully satisfied.

Catherine: All that matters to me is you. Now that you have returned safely I am relieved.

CHAPTER 11

Two hearts beats in unionism
When soul and mind finds a reason.
Dreams of when they will be one
Forever to hold the precious find.

Lorenzo experienced total peace and quiet on entering Catherine's residence. He exclaimed, "Catherine I needed this sort of atmosphere to relax and rest after three months of hectic engagements. I am glad you brought me to your residence. You know at my residence the scenario will be different."

"Yes, I know. They will celebrate your success by partying and having a lot of fun. Your whole family, Lorenzo, is very loving, very special. They all love you very much and so do you in return. They grab every opportunity to praise you. Never do they get tired of praising you. They all have a very special place for you in their heart and life. Besides you Lorenzo, I am equally fortunate to have such a loving, caring family.

"Every member of your family has accepted me wholeheartedly. I feel honoured by their love and generosity extended to me right from the start of our relationship. I still remember the first time you took me to your residence, I was so nervous that I forgot my name and started sweating, not knowing what to say. Belinda, your sister, who sensed my trouble, rushed towards me and announced my name as Catherine Pelagio. Belinda then escorted me inside the house and helped me to calm down, followed by your mother Isabela, who comforted me further. I really consider myself as very fortunate to have such loving in-laws."

Lorenzo and Catherine decided to make the most of this opportunity while residing at Catherine's residence to discuss their future course of action. Catherine had marriage on her mind but was hesitating to bring up the topic at this stage, as Lorenzo had just returned from a very busy trip abroad. But then the issue of implementing the business plan would have to be given top priority, as delays would derail the implementation process.

Catherine decided to consult her father on this important issue as he was better equipped with experience to guide her in such matters. Stefano Pelagio, after a great deal of thought, ruled his decision in Lorenzo's favour. Catherine was delighted with her father's decision since she too had felt that it was the right thing to do.

Catherine is very thrilled to be in the company of Lorenzo. The very thought of him delights her. She gets lost in thoughts of him in a dream world even though she is wide awake, but is unconscious of her surroundings. When she gets caught daydreaming she blushes and shies away to her bedroom.

As she continued to dwell in her romantic dream world, Lorenzo entered the balcony where she was seated and kept staring at her, not knowing what she was staring at or why she was motionless.

Just then, Stefano Pelagio started watering the garden plants and noticed his daughter in a static state and Lorenzo staring at her, puzzled and confused. Stefano Pelagio rushed to the balcony and explained the situation. Lorenzo moved towards her, touched her shoulder and called her name. Catherine at once sprang to her feet and felt embarrassed. She embraced him, resting her head on his chest. Holding each other, they entered Catherine's room and settled on a sofa. She continued to rest her head on Lorenzo's shoulder, holding him tight.

Lorenzo: What were you dreaming?

Catherine: I dream about you only when I am not with you. That is how I pass my time, dreaming. When I got up this morning I walked in your room and found you in deep sleep. I sat on your bed and kissed you. I didn't want to disturb your sleep as you need to rest. I sat and stared at you for a long time. You are so handsome and peaceful in your sleep. Staring at you, time passed swiftly as I got totally engrossed, dreaming of our future.

Lorenzo: Let's not worry about the future. At present we deserve a good vacation. Don't you think so Catherine?

Catherine: Yes, I totally agree with you. I haven't had one for quite some time. It will do you a lot of good Lorenzo, so Let us get working out the details of our vacation.

Just then Stefano Pelagio showed up with a broad smile and said, "Guess what I am up to this time?"

"Are you going for a swim at Camaro de Lobos beach which is your favourite pastime?"

"No not at all. I have booked a month's holiday for both of you to relax and recuperate in Venice."

"Oh Dad you are always full of surprises. Venice is a very romantic place and I always dreamed of visiting it. Oh Dad you are so thoughtful. You always give me pleasant surprises when I least expect it. I am so thrilled that I can't wait to be there. By the way, why visit Venice of all the places in the world? Surely you must have a good reason."

"Yes Catherine, you are right, I do have a very good reason. Your mother and I visited Venice for our honeymoon. Since then, we visited Venice every year on our wedding anniversary till she passed away. Since then I never visited Venice. You were too young then."

"I am so sorry, Dad. You must be missing her so much, even now."

"Yes I do miss her and remember her always, especially our trips to Venice. All I have now is her sweet memories, you, and Lorenzo to live on. You have one week's time for your departure, so start packing all your requirements to leave for Venice."

CHAPTER 12

Enjoy your life while you are a free bird,
Make the most of your freedom,
Before taking the plunge
Think how deep or steep is the climb.

A week later Catherine and Lorenzo left for Venice. Stefano Pelagio and Lorenzo's family wished them a pleasant vacation and saw them off at the airport. Verona is one of the most enchanting cities in Northern Italy. Verona is a romantic paradise on Earth. The quiet cloisters, old ancient streets, palaces, gardens – every bit of Verona is romantic as any visitor would expect, and so did Catherine and Lorenzo from Portugal, since it is Romeo and Juliet's city. Catherine and Lorenzo have a special place for Venice in their heart because of the long association with Venice for generations together. And now that they are here, they want to make their visit a memorable one.

Lorenzo and Catherine hired a tour guide, Mr Marco Valerio, since this is their first visit to Venice. Mr Marco Valerio is a very friendly, cheerful, elderly person who loves what he is doing, meeting people and being of service to them. Marco started the exploration of Venice with his two companions by visiting first the Baroque Santo Maria della Salute Church at the mouth of the Grand Canal, where the banks of the Venice's busy main watercourse are filled with beautiful buildings best viewed from a gondola.

Gondolas are now largely used as pleasure craft for tourists, which gives a very pleasant perspective of the city, riding past grand palatial homes using an old route that dates back many centuries. Followed by Giardino Giusti, hidden among the dusty facades at the entrance to one of Italy's finest Renaissance Gardens. Laid out in 1580, one of Italy's finest Renaissance gardens attracted the attention of Lorenzo and Catherine so much that they got totally lost in the beautiful settings. Verona was an ancient Roman stronghold famous as the home of the lovers Romeo and Juliet. Verona today is a city of opera, theatre, and art.

Today Catherine and Lorenzo are visiting the house of Juliet Casa di Giulietta. The tragic story of Romeo and Juliet written by Luigi da Porto of Vicenza in the 1520s inspired countless poems, films, ballets, and dramas. At the Casa di Giulietta (Juliet's house, No. 27 via Cappello), Romeo climbed Juliet's balcony. The run-down Casa di Romeo is in via delle Arche Scaligere, while the Tomba di Giulietta is in a crypt below the cloister of San Francesco al Corso on via del Pontiere. The stone sarcophagus is empty and rather plain, but the setting is atmospheric. At Montecchio Maggiore visitors come especially to view the two fourteenth-century castles on the hill above the town. These are known as the Castello di Romeo and Castello di Giulietta.

Catherine could not hold back her tears thinking of their tragic death. Some people do cry when they are overcome with grief, especially if they too have gone through a similar experience. She wondered during that era why lovers were treated harshly, as if loving somebody is a crime in itself. Romeo and Juliet showed what true love is. In the history of humanity there is no parallel to such a unique love story. Catherine and Lorenzo vowed at the tomb of Juliet to live in love for the rest of their lives.

Next they visited the Arena. Verona's amphitheatre, completed around AD 30, is the third largest in the world. Sant'Anastacia Church, a huge one, was begun in 1290 and built to hold a massive congregation, across the Ponte Romano (Roman Bridge) that links Verona city centre. This upmarket residential district is dotted with fine palaces, gardens and churches and offers good view back onto the towers and domes of the medieval city. Basilica San Marco is crowned with five huge domes and is a must-see piece of great architecture. St Mark's body, believed lost in the fire of AD 976, supposedly reappeared when the new church was consecrated in 1094. The remains are housed in the altar. On the last leg of their holidays they hired the Lady Anne Yacht at San Marco Canal to end their tour of a memorable holiday. Travelling by a voporetto or waterbus is fun, via the Grand Canal, to admire the beautiful natural setting. They took the return flight home, happy and satisfied with their wonderful vacation.

*

Lorenzo outsourced the entire plan approved by

the management to contractors and appointed Antonio J. Rebeiro, his brother, to manage the entire business operation in his absence while he and Catherine were holidaying in Venice. Antonio accepted the offer and assured Lorenzo that he would do his best to be the best, like Lorenzo. Antonio called a meeting of all the management core group members to roll into action the process of implementing the approved plan. He delegated assignment to all core group members. Each core group member had to check their respective field of expertise to see that the work carried out met the agreed level of sophistication from the contractors.

Romeo and Susanna paid a surprise visit to Lorenzo and Catherine to catch up with them the latest happenings. Lorenzo and Catherine spoke at length of their wonderful experience of the city of Venice. Catherine let the cat out of her bag and surprised everybody by announcing the wedding plans of Belinda, Lorenzo's only sister. This news surprised everyone as all in the family were expecting wedding bells to ring for Lorenzo and Catherine first. Stunned family members focused their gaze on Lorenzo, so he made a statement to clear the suspense.

"Belinda is our only sister. To get her married first is our tradition and custom and that is not all. I had promised to my father that I'll not marry till I get my only sister married first. I am keeping my promise and also doing my duty as the elder brother in the absence of my father."

On hearing Lorenzo speak the way he did, tears rolled down their cheeks in an emotionally charged atmosphere. All present hugged and kissed him for his noble nature, especially Belinda, who found it difficult to stop crying. Women-folk of the house escorted Belinda and helped her to calm down.

Francisco, Lorenzo's best childhood friend, accepted the proposal from the elders of the Ribeiro family to marry Belinda Ribeiro. Wedding preparations began in earnest with excitement writ large on their smiling faces.

Romance fills the air and the would-be couple and family are totally engrossed in planning first the spiritual part of the wedding, which forms the most important part of a marriage blessed by a priest in matrimony.

Belinda, who teaches catechism for children in the church, shouldered the responsibility of all the wedding's spiritual matters, including the choir, altar decoration with fresh flowers, candles, incense, cushions, mats, curtains, holy water, and altar boys. Antonio shouldered the wedding reception, guest list, wedding costumes, catering, limousine, toast master, and free transportation to the reception venue for guests at Reid's Palace Hotel, Funchal.

Camaro de Lobos village began buzzing with activity and excitement. Weddings, by nature, are very romantic. They stir up feelings of romance in every heart whether young or old. Youngsters secretly do their best to find their best mate and when they find one, grab the first opportunity in a romance-filled atmosphere to introduce their heartthrob to the family. Older couples do not lag behind in romance. Age may have caught up with them but their hearts are young still vibrant and full of life. That's the best way to live long.

*

Francisco and Belinda are preparing for the big occasion. They are excited but nervous too, since this is the first time they will be marching towards the aisle to say 'I DO', and they both will be the centre of attention and scrutiny of all present for the occasion. They have rehearsed their vows and the gospel readings so they may deliver them with perfection. Friends and relatives are working behind the scenes to ensure everything moves according to plan. Lorenzo provided for the needs of the less fortunate to look their best for the wedding so that they could attend the wedding feeling honoured and accepted. After complying with all the local customs, it is time for them to get married.

The sun is shining, the sky is clear and blue, a perfect day for a perfect wedding. Camaro de Lobos village came alive with decorations and lights, giving it a festive look seen never before. The church was painted white and lit with decorative lights for the occasion. Guests, family members and friends started arriving at the Church of Sao Sebastiao, Canical, Camara, for the nuptial mass. The church was packed to capacity. Lorenzo did the honour of the best man and Catherine the bridesmaid.

The spiritual church ceremony went as planned without a hitch and the groom and bride, after signing the marriage register, heaved a sigh of relief. After the crowd finished congratulating the groom and bride, all proceeded to the Reid's Palace Hotel for the final celebration of dancing and dining.

The bride and groom's families were full of smiles and praise for the wonderful wedding they witnessed.

They returned home with a grateful heart, thanking all who worked tirelessly to make the wedding celebration a memorable one. Lorenzo kept his promise and married his only sister with a grand celebration never witnessed in the history of Camaro de Lobos village. The memory of this wedding has left a lasting impression on all those who witnessed it. Francisco and Belinda began their married life at Francisco's residence.

CHAPTER 13

Love is the sweet essence of life.

Lorenzo has been very successful in achieving all that he set out to do. He is no longer the same Lorenzo people knew him once.

Now it is Lorenzo's turn to tie the knot to marry his sweetheart, Catherine Pelagio. The long wait is almost over. Lorenzo and Catherine are preparing for their wedding. Once again both families are buzzing with activity. The whole of Camara de Lobos village is excited. Wedding invitation cards are distributed personally by Lorenzo and Catherine to all. Reids Palace Hotel, Funchal, is the venue for the wedding celebration. Lorenzo and Catherine were all smiles and so were all the family members and invited guests, and especially the whole of Camaro de Lobos village.

In the presence of all family members, relatives, friends, and invited guests, Lorenzo and Catherine exchanged their marriage vows and sealed their love and life forever by saying, "I DO."

CPSIA information can be obtained
at www.ICGtesting.com
Printed in the USA
LVHW081721270120
644931LV00042B/2930